Dear Parent:

Congratulations! Your child is taking the first steps on an exciting journey. The destination? Independent reading!

STEP INTO READING® will help your child get there. The program offers five steps to reading success. Each step includes fun stories and colorful art. There are also Step into Reading Sticker Books, Step into Reading Math Readers, Step into Reading Phonics Readers, Step into Reading Write-In Readers, and Step into Reading Phonics Boxed Sets—a complete literacy program with something for every child.

Learning to Read, Step by Step!

Ready to Read   Preschool–Kindergarten
• big type and easy words • rhyme and rhythm • picture clues
For children who know the alphabet and are eager to begin reading.

Reading with Help   Preschool–Grade 1
• basic vocabulary • short sentences • simple stories
For children who recognize familiar words and sound out new words with help.

Reading on Your Own   Grades 1–3
• engaging characters • easy-to-follow plots • popular topics
For children who are ready to read on their own.

Reading Paragraphs   Grades 2–3
• challenging vocabulary • short paragraphs • exciting stories
For newly independent readers who read simple sentences with confidence.

Ready for Chapters   Grades 2–4
• chapters • longer paragraphs • full-color art
For children who want to take the plunge into chapter books but still like colorful pictures.

STEP INTO READING® is designed to give every child a successful reading experience. The grade levels are only guides. Children can progress through the steps at their own speed, developing confidence in their reading, no matter what their grade.

Remember, a lifetime love of reading starts with a single step!

Originally published separately as *Big Snowman, Little Snowman,* copyright © 2013 Disney Enterprises, Inc.; *A Tale of Two Sisters,* copyright © 2013 Disney Enterprises, Inc.; *Anna's Best Friends,* copyright © 2014 Disney Enterprises, Inc.; *Hello, Olaf!,* copyright © 2015 Disney Enterprises, Inc.; *Across the Sea,* copyright © 2016 Disney Enterprises, Inc.; *The Right Track,* copyright © 2017 Disney Enterprises, Inc.; and *Ghost Hunt!,* copyright © 2018 Disney Enterprises, Inc.

Step into Reading, Random House, and the Random House colophon are registered trademarks of Penguin Random House LLC.

Visit us on the Web!
StepIntoReading.com
rhcbooks.com

Educators and librarians, for a variety of teaching tools, visit us at RHTeachersLibrarians.com

ISBN 978-0-7364-4089-9

August 2019

MANUFACTURED IN CHINA
10 9 8 7 6 5 4 3 2

SEVEN MAGICAL TALES

A Collection of Seven Early Readers

Random House 🏠 New York

CONTENTS

Meet the Characters

ELSA

❄ Queen of Arendelle

❄ Best friend and sister to Anna

❄ Has the power to control ice and snow

❄ Quote: "LET IT GO!"

Anna

- Princess of Arendelle
- Best friend and sister to Elsa
- Loves to dance, sing, and dream
- Quote: "DO YOU WANT TO BUILD A SNOWMAN?"

OLAF

❄ Magical snowman made by Elsa

❄ Enjoys making new friends

❄ Loves spending time in the sun

❄ Quote: "I'M OLAF, AND
I LIKE WARM HUGS!"

KRISTOFF

✻ Harvests ice from the mountain lakes

✻ Best friend is his reindeer, Sven

✻ Grew up with magical trolls

✻ Quote: "ICE IS MY LIFE!"

SVEN

* Loyal reindeer to best friend, Kristoff
* Pulls wooden sled full of supplies
* Loves to eat carrots
* Enjoys icy adventures

MARSHMALLOW

- ❄ Huge magical snowman
- ❄ Protects Queen Elsa's ice palace
- ❄ Scares off unwelcome guests
- ❄ Quote: "GO AWAY!"

HANS

❄ Prince of the Southern Isles

❄ Youngest of 13 brothers

❄ Biggest goal is to be king

❄ Quote: "I LOVE CRAZY!"

TROLLS

- Live in a valley near Arendelle
- Raised Kristoff and Sven
- Able to change into rocks at will
- Quote: "KRISTOFF'S HOME!"

STEP INTO READING®

STEP 1 READY TO READ

DISNEY

FROZEN

BIG SNOWMAN, LITTLE SNOWMAN

by Tish Rabe
illustrated by the Disney Storybook Art Team

Random House 🏠 New York

HAPPY sister.

SAD sister.

At first,

Hans seems nice.

Elsa runs away.
She makes the
snow and ice!

26

Anna gets ON her horse.
Ride, Anna, ride!

Anna falls OFF.

It's cold outside.

Anna meets Kristoff.

His reindeer is Sven.

Kristoff goes IN . . .

then OUT again!

Anna and Kristoff
go, go, go!
Sven climbs FAST.

Anna climbs SLOW.

Elsa has a palace.

Anna enters FIRST.

Kristoff enters LAST.

Elsa freezes Anna
with an icy blast!

COLD Olaf dreams
of the HOT, HOT sun.

LITTLE snowman.

BIG snowman!

Run! Run! Run!

Anna is freezing.

She is worried, too.

She asks a troll
what to do.

Watch out!
Hans attacks!

Anna is in FRONT.

Elsa is in BACK.

Winter ENDS.

Summer STARTS.

Anna's act of love
has thawed
her frozen heart.

Olaf APART.

Sisters TOGETHER.

Elsa, Anna, and Olaf . . .

friends forever!

STEP INTO READING®

STEP 2
READING WITH HELP

DISNEY
FROZEN

A Tale of Two Sisters

by Melissa Lagonegro

illustrated by Maria Elena Naggi, Studio Iboix,
and the Disney Storybook Art Team

Random House 🏠 New York

Princess Elsa
and Princess Anna
are sisters.

Elsa has a secret.

She has magic powers.

She can create ice.

Elsa makes a mistake.
Her magic hits Anna.
Anna is very cold.
Their parents worry.

Anna gets warm again.
She wants to be friends
with her big sister.

To keep Anna safe,

Elsa stays away.

It makes Elsa sad.

Anna and Elsa grow up.

Anna meets Prince Hans.

They fall in love.

Elsa becomes queen.

The kingdom cheers.

Anna wants
to marry Hans.
Elsa says no.
Anna and Elsa argue.
Anna pulls off
Elsa's glove.

Magic ice shoots
from Elsa's hand.

Elsa runs far away.
She does not want
her magic
to hurt anyone.

Elsa covers the land
with snow.
She makes an ice palace.

The kingdom needs Elsa
to stop the storm.
There is so much snow!
Anna must find Elsa.

Anna meets Kristoff
and his reindeer, Sven.
They help her search
for Elsa.

They meet Olaf.

He is a nice snowman.

He leads them to Elsa.

The kingdom worries
about Anna.

Hans will find her.

Anna finally finds Elsa.
She tells Elsa
to come home.

Elsa is afraid
she might hurt someone.
Anna will not listen.

Elsa grows angry.
She blasts Anna
with a bolt of ice.

Elsa makes
a giant snowman.
He chases
Anna and her friends
out of the palace.

Elsa's blast is turning
Anna to ice!
An old troll helps Anna.

He says an act
of true love
can save her.

Hans finds Elsa.
His guards
bring her home.

Hans will not kiss Anna.

He does not love her.

He just wants

to rule the kingdom.

Anna is almost frozen.

Kristoff loves Anna.

His kiss might save her.

But Elsa needs Anna's help!

Hans tries to hurt Elsa.
Anna blocks his sword
when she freezes solid.

Elsa is safe.

She cries.

She hugs Anna.

Anna starts to melt!
Her act of love
has saved their lives.

The sisters
are best friends
at last!

DISNEY

FROZEN

ANNA'S BEST FRIENDS

by Christy Webster

illustrated by the Disney Storybook Art Team

Random House 🏠 New York

Olaf the snowman

is Anna's friend.

He dreams
of warmer weather.

Reindeer Sven is

Kristoff's friend.

They always
stick together.

A frozen adventure
in a sleigh.

Run, Sven, run!

Get away!

Anna explores
the ice and snow.

Her friends tell her
which way to go.

Anna's sister, Elsa,

makes magical ice.

Sometimes sisters disagree.

Sometimes they are nice.

Sven is brave.
He pulls the sled
higher.

Olaf is brave.

He builds Anna a fire.

Now Anna's adventures
are done.

She and her friends have
some fun!

Elsa, Kristoff,
Olaf, and Sven.

They will always be Anna's best friends!

$Disney$

FROZEN

HELLO, OLAF!

by Andrea Posner-Sanchez

Random House 🏠 New York

This is Olaf.

He is a snowman.

Elsa made a snowman
to play with when she
was a little girl.
Elsa and Anna called
the snowman Olaf.
They pretended he
was alive.

Years later, Elsa uses
her magical powers
to really make Olaf
come to life!

Anna is all
grown up now.
Olaf meets Anna,
Kristoff, and Sven.

Sven loves carrots.

Olaf better hold on
to his nose!

Olaf wishes for warm days and sunshine.

A day on the beach
would be a dream
come true!

118

Olaf would sail.

Olaf would swim.

He would even sit
in a hot tub.
Do not melt, Olaf!

Elsa has a way
to keep Olaf cold
even when it is warm.

She does some magic.

Now Olaf the snowman
will never melt!

ACROSS THE SEA

by Ruth Homberg

based on the original story by Brittany Candau

illustrated by the Disney Storybook Art Team

Random House 🏠 New York

Elsa and Anna are going
on a trip!
They will set sail
to see new places.

Elsa packs.
Anna looks
out the window.
The ship is ready!

Anna steers the ship.
Elsa looks
at the map.

Elsa uses her magic.

She makes a strong wind
to fill the sails.

Land ho!

Soon they arrive
in a new kingdom.
Elsa and Anna meet
the king and queen.

They try new foods.

They see new kinds

of flowers.

The king and queen
throw a party
for Anna and Elsa.

Anna learns
a new dance.

Anna and Elsa
visit another kingdom.
Elsa sees art
with the queen.

Anna plays
with a funny animal!

The queen shows Elsa
a block of ice.
She asks Elsa
to carve
an ice sculpture.

Will Elsa use her magic?

Elsa is too shy.

Anna carves a snowman

in the ice.

It looks like Olaf!

Anna and Elsa
visit another city.
They see the Duke!

The city is very hot.
The Duke does not
like the heat.

Anna and Elsa walk
with the Duke.
Everyone in the city
is hot and sticky.

Elsa wants to help.

She uses her magic.

It starts to snow!

The people cheer!

Elsa makes

frosty drinks.

Everyone feels better.

Even the Duke is happy.

Anna and Elsa
ride sleds.
People ice-skate.

Anna is proud of Elsa.
She sprays the Duke
with snow!
Brrr!

It is time to sail home.
Anna and Elsa wave
goodbye to their
new friends.
They had such a fun trip
across the sea!

Disney

FROZEN

NORTHERN LIGHTS

THE RIGHT TRACK

adapted by Apple Jordan
based on the original story by Suzanne Francis
illustrated by the Disney Storybook Art Team

Random House 🏠 New York

Kristoff and his friends
are going
to Troll Valley.

Tomorrow is
the Crystal Ceremony.
They will help
the trolls celebrate!

A troll named Little Rock
greets them.

Little Rock is sad.
His tracking crystal
will not glow.
He cannot be
in the ceremony
if he is not
a good tracker.

Grand Pabbie is gone!

"Let's track him,"

says Kristoff.

Little Rock agrees.

He will find Grand Pabbie
and make his
tracking crystal glow!

The friends set off
on their journey.
Little Rock
leads the way.

Little Rock picks
up a scent.
He thinks it is
Grand Pabbie!
But it is only Sven.

The friends climb
a large mountain.
Anna and Elsa
tell stories.

They help Little Rock

feel brave.

Soon they come
to a frozen river.
They try to cross.
The ice cracks!

Little Rock almost
falls in.
Kristoff and Anna
help him.

Elsa waves her arms.
She makes a stairway
of ice.

It stretches
across the river.

Little Rock and Olaf
run down the steps.
The steps begin
to fall.

Elsa uses her magic.

She makes ice sleds.

The friends jump on.
They race across
the frozen river.

Little Rock thanks his
friends for saving him.
He shares a crystal
with Anna and Elsa.

They know Little Rock
will soon light
his tracking crystal, too . . .

. . . even if he needs
a little help
from his friends!

FROZEN

GHOST HUNT!

adapted by Melissa Lagonegro
based on the original story by Victoria Saxon
illustrated by the Disney Storybook Art Team

Random House 🏠 New York

Anna and Elsa are having
a slumber party!
Olaf brings a ghost story
to read.

Elsa gets snacks.

Anna gets pillows
and blankets.

They find a cozy spot.
They eat their snacks.
Elsa reads
the ghost story.

Anna falls asleep.

Elsa yawns.

But Olaf is not tired.

Olaf wants
to find a ghost.
He goes
on a ghost hunt!

Olaf searches
the dark castle.
He cannot find a ghost.

<u>Thump!</u> <u>Crash!</u>
Olaf falls down
the stairs!

Anna and Elsa
hear a noise.
They wake up.

Elsa lights a candle.
The sisters search
the dark halls.

Anna and Elsa look
down the stairs.

They see a ghost!

Anna and Elsa go closer.
"We want to be friends,"
says Anna.

"Me too!"
says the ghost.
"Do you like
warm hugs?"

Elsa pulls
off the sheet.
It is not a ghost.
It is Olaf!

Olaf did not
find a ghost.
He <u>was</u> a ghost!